DINOSAURS

Richard Walker

Triceratops

A Golden Guide from St. Martin's Press

Tyrannosaurus skull

Euoplocephalus

Brachiosaurus

Parasaurolophus skeleton

Troodon tooth

DINOSAURS

A Golden Photo Guide from St. Martin's Press

Stegosaurus

St. Martin's Press
New York
Manufactured in China

Produced by
Elm Grove Books Limited

Series Editor Susie Elwes
Text Editor Angela Wilkes
Art Director Louise Morley
Illustration John Woodcock
Picture Research
Claire Gouldstone
Models created by Martin Baker,
Dougal Dixon, Graham High
Index Hilary Bird

Original Edition © 2000
Image Quest Limited
This edition © 2001
Elm Grove Books Limited

**St. Martin's Press
175 Fifth Avenue
New York N.Y. 10010.
www.stmartins.com**

A CIP catalogue record for this
book is available from the
Library of Congress

ISBN 1-58238-175-5

Text and Photographs in this book
previously published in
Eyewitness 3D Dinosaurs

This edition published 2001

ACKNOWLEDGMENTS
Ardea :Title, /John Daniels 42tr, David Dixon 15tr, Kenneth W. Fink 20b, Francois Gohier 9br, 18t, 20t, 30t, 30bl, 36l
Clem Haagner 16bl P. Morris 10b, 43tr; **Bruce Coleman Collection** 37 tr; **Corbis/Hulton-Deutsch Collection** 45br;
Dorling Kindersley: Title, 3b, 6/7t, 9bl, 16 main, 19bl, 24l, 25br, 27b, 31b, 43bl, Andrew Crawford 1, 4b, 9t, 18b, 32l, 39r/
Royal Tyrell Museum of Palaeontology, Canada 6tl, 7b, 8tl, 25bl, 29tl; **FLPA**/ Brake/Sunset 52r, GP Eaton 52l, Eichhorn/Zingel 35b,
AR Hamblin 40/41t, Gerard Lacz 4t, S. McCutcheon 53tr, Philip Perry 26b, W. Roholich 33tl, Tony Wharton 13tr, R. Wilmhurst 53b;
John Gurche: 33, 51; **Hammer/The Kobal Collection** 15bl; **Museum of the Rockies, Montana** 33b; **Natural History
Museum, London**: Title, 3t, 5b, 12b, 15br, 17b, 19c, 19t, 19r, 24r, 26tl, 28t, 28b, 29b, 29c, 31c, 31tr, 34bl, 35c, 38r, 40tl, 40b, 41t,
41bl, 41br, 41c, 42tl, 42b, 43br, 44b, 43c, 45c, 45cr, 46t, 47bl, 47br, 47c, 48l, 49c, 50l, 54t, 55b, 56b, 57r, Index, John Sibbick 6b, 13br,
14b, 26t, 32b, 36c, 36r, 38l, 58b, Index; **Peabody Museum of Natural History, Yale University** 34br, 51; **R.E.H. Reid** 23bl,
23br; **Science Photo Library** 44t, 45bl, Peter Menzel 49c, 49b, Tom McHugh 5tl, 37b, /Alfred Pasieka 11tr, Philippe Plailly 48b,
/Francois Sauze 30br; **Kim Taylor**:5c, 7c, 9c, 1c, 13c, 15c, 17c, 21c, 23c, 25,c, 27c, 37c, 39c, 53c; **Tony Stone Images** 21br

Pachycephalosaurus skull

CONTENTS

Compsognathus

DINOSAURS DEFINED

CROCODILE COUSINS
This Nile crocodile, a predator that hunts animals on riverbanks and in the water, is similar in looks and lifestyle to crocodilians that lived at the same time as the dinosaurs.

Dinosaurs were extraordinary reptiles that appeared about 230 million years ago (mya) and died out 65 mya. Like all reptiles, they had waterproof, scaly skin and young that hatched from eggs. However, unlike other reptiles, dinosaurs stood upright. Other reptiles that lived at the same time included crocodilians, flying pterosaurs, and plesiosaurs in the sea. These, however, were not dinosaurs.

Stegosaurus may have used its large back plates to help it to defend itself.

STEGOSAURUS
As long as a coach and as heavy as a rhinoceros, this dinosaur lived in North America about 150 mya. A plant-eater, it cropped leaves with its horned beak. It defended itself with its spiky tail.

A giant of the air, Pteranodon had a wingspan of up to 23 feet (7 m).

IN THE FOREST

These dinosaurs lived about 113 mya and they were very different from each other. The larger one is *Iguanodon*, a plant-eater that browsed on leafy vegetation. *Deinonychus*, the smaller dinosaur, was a fierce, meat-eating predator with sharp claws and teeth.

FLYING REPTILES

Pterosaurs were the first vertebrates – animals with backbones – to actively fly. Their long wings, supported by their arm bones and elongated finger bones, were made of skin. *Pteranodon* probably caught insects on the wing, or scooped up fish from the sea with its long, toothless beak.

SEA REPTILES

Sea-living reptiles included plesiosaurs like this one, and the fish-shaped ichthyosaurs. Like other marine reptiles, plesiosaurs breathed air. They were all carnivores, and fed on fish and other marine animals.

LIZARD HIPS

Ilium

Pubis points forward.

Ischium points backward.

Dinosaurs fall into two main groups – lizard-hipped or bird-hipped – depending on the structure of their hip girdle. The hip girdle connected the hind legs to the backbone. In lizard-hipped, or saurischian, dinosaurs, the pubis bones pointed forward, as they do in lizards. This group included the carnivorous dinosaurs, or theropods; and a group of large herbivorous dinosaurs, the sauropods, and their relatives.

LIZARD HIP
This side view from the right shows one half of the hip girdle of a lizard-hipped dinosaur. The pubis and ilium bones clearly point forward, while the ischium points backward.

Apatosaurus *was tall enough to feed on treetops.*

GIANT SAUROPOD
Apatosaurus was a typical sauropod: it had a large body and four pillar-like legs, a long neck, a small head, and a long whiplike tail that could be used to lash out against enemies.

A small theropod, showing the position of its hip bones.

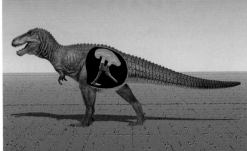

GIANT HIPS

This giant meat-eater, like other theropods, walked on its hind legs. Its hip girdle was massive to support the dinosaur's enormous weight on its hind legs.

Long tail helped the dinosaur to balance as it ran.

Toothless beak and long, flexible neck.

The hip girdle connects the long, slender legs to the rest of the body.

ORNITHOMIMUS SKELETON

This high-speed dinosaur belonged to a group of dinosaurs that resembled modern ostriches. *Ornithomimus* used its long legs to escape from predators. It was an omnivore and used its sharp-edged, toothless beak to feed on either small animals or fruit.

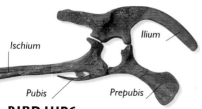

Ischium

Ilium

Pubis

Prepubis

BIRD HIPS

All dinosaurs had three paired hip bones connecting the hind legs to the backbone. In bird-hipped dinosaurs – as in modern birds – the pubis and the ischium bones both pointed backward in the same direction, as they do in this ornithopod hip girdle.

ARMOR PLATING

Euoplocephalus was an ankylosaur or armored dinosaur. Its tough, leathery hide was studded with bony nodules and shoulder spikes, it had bony plates on its head, and a club at the end of its tail with which to ward off attackers.

BIRD HIPS

The bird-hipped, or ornithischian, dinosaurs had a different hip girdle from the lizard-hipped dinosaurs. All of them were hoofed herbivores and most of them had beaked mouths. Some of them walked on two legs and others on four. There were five groups of bird-hipped dinosaurs: ornithopods, stegosaurs, ankylosaurs, pachycephalosaurs, and ceratopians.

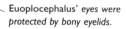

Euoplocephalus' eyes were protected by bony eyelids.

Bird-hipped
Stegosaurus'
hip girdle

_Thick,
domed skull_

_Short arms
and small
hands_

IGUANODON

The arrangement of its hip bones show that _Iguanodon_ was a bird-hipped dinosaur. It was about twice the height of a human and could walk on its hind legs or, when looking for food, on all fours.

BONE HEAD

Stegoceras was a pachycephalosaur. Like all pachycephalosaurs, it walked on its hind legs and had a thick, domed skull that may have been used to head-butt rivals.

BONY FRILL

The large bony loops at the back of this _Chasmosaurus_ skull supported a huge neck frill that was typical of many ceratopians. The head of this stocky, 16 ft (5 m) long dinosaur was also armed with horns.

FIRST DINOSAURS

During the Triassic Period about 248–205 mya, reptiles flourished and dominated life on land. The most successful reptile group, which appeared about 230 mya, was the dinosaurs. A key factor in their success was the way their legs stood directly under their bodies, supporting their whole weight. This meant they could walk farther, move faster, and grow bigger than other reptiles whose legs were spread out on either side of their bodies.

TRIASSIC EARTH

During the Triassic Period, there was a single landmass, called Pangaea. The climate was dry and warm or hot, and dinosaurs rapidly colonized the landmass.

SPRAWLING LEGS

This skeleton of *Dimetrodon*, an early reptile that lived before the dinosaurs some 270 mya, has a sprawling posture that can still be seen in lizards today. Their legs were not directly under their bodies and could not support a heavy weight. They could not move far or fast.

Sprawling legs only provide limited support for the body.

EUPARKARIA

This early Triassic reptile was among the ancestors of the dinosaurs, crocodilians, and pterosaurs. *Euparkaria* was supported by legs that were partly beneath its body in a semi-sprawling stance.

Legs stick out, and bend slightly at the knees to lift the body clear of the ground.

OLD TREE

The ginkgo tree is the sole remaining species of a group of plants that were common during the Triassic Period. Conifers and seed ferns also thrived.

SEMI-SPRAWLING LEGS

Early Triassic dinosaur ancestors used semi-sprawling legs to move more efficiently over short distances. Living crocodiles also do this. They sprawl when walking, but raise their bodies to run fast.

STANDING TALL

Dinosaurs, such as this *Triceratops*, stood upright. It was this posture that enabled dinosaurs to grow bigger, move faster, and adopt many lifestyles.

Straight legs standing directly under the body support weight most efficiently.

JURASSIC WORLD

In the Jurassic Period, 205–144 mya, the climate was warm and moist, creating ideal conditions for plants to grow. Lush vegetation provided plenty of food for plant-eating dinosaurs, which increased in numbers, varieties, and size. Large carnivorous dinosaurs, all theropods, evolved to prey on the many different herbivores; smaller theropods hunted insects and small animals.

JURASSIC EARTH

During the Jurassic Period, the single super-continent, Pangaea, broke into two continents: Laurasia in the north, and Gondwana in the south.

The form of the arms suggests Heterodontosaurus could dig for tubers and insects.

HETERODONTOSAURUS

This small dinosaur, whose name means mixed-tooth lizard, was a plant-eater and grazed on low-growing, tough vegetation. If threatened by a predator, it sprinted away on its hind legs at high speed.

JURASSIC BROWSER

At the lakeside *Apatosaurus*, a large sauropod, stretched its long neck up to browse on treetops and down to eat low-growing ferns and horsetails. Tall conifers, such as pines, smaller tree ferns, ginkgoes, and cycads were common during the Jurassic Period.

HORSETAILS

These modern plants are descendants of ancient horsetails that flourished, together with ferns, on the damp, swampy Jurassic plains.

THE FIRST MAMMALS

Early mammals, such as this *Megazostrodon,* were small, nocturnal insect-eaters. They probably laid eggs but fed their young on milk. Mammals remained small until the dinosaurs became extinct 65 mya.

Stegosaurus   *Apatosaurus*

The long tail acted as a counterbalance.

YANGCHUANOSAURUS

This large carnivorous dinosaur, found in China, was about 29 ft 6 in (9 m) long and lived in the late Jurassic period. *Yangchuanosaurus* was an allosaur. Its prey may have included young sauropods.

CRETACEOUS WORL[

During the Cretaceous Period, 144–65 mya, dinosaurs on different continents evolved separately and became more diverse. Over half the dinosaurs we know about today lived during the Cretaceous, including the horned ceratopians, the duck-billed hadrosaurs, the armored ankylosaurs, and the giant carnivore *Tyrannosaurus*. By the end of the Cretaceous, dinosaurs had become extinct.

CHANGING WORLD

The two landmasses moved farther apart during the Cretaceous to form continents whose shapes resemble those today. Parts of North America and Europe were covered by shallow seas. Africa, India, South America, Antarctica, and Australia moved apart.

The hand had five digits, including a thumb spike.

MUTTABURRASAURUS

This relative of *Iguanodon* lived in Australia. *Muttaburrasaurus* was about 23 ft (7 m) long and walked on either its hind legs or on all fours. It used its toothless beak to crop plants.

THE LAST DINOSAURS

The three-horned dinosaur *Triceratops* snipped up plants with its parrotlike beak. It belonged to the group of horned dinosaurs called ceratopians. *Triceratops* was one of the last dinosaurs to become extinct at the end of the Cretaceous Period.

IMPOSSIBLE SCENE?

The film *One Million Years BC* showed the impossible: humans and dinosaurs living at the same time. Modern humans only appeared about 300,000 years ago.

Modern magnolia

FLOWERING PLANTS

During the Cretaceous Period, plants with flowers such as the magnolia, appeared for the first time.

Slashing claw

FIERCE HUNTERS

Packs of ferocious *Deinonychus*, whose name means terrible claw, preyed on large plant-eating dinosaurs. Another fierce hunter was the later giant *Tyrannosaurus*.

GIANTS AND MIDGETS

A long neck enabled this dinosaur to reach leaves at any level.

GIANT

Brachiosaurus was one of the biggest dinosaurs 75 ft (23 m) long and as tall as a house. This massive plant-eater was supported by pillarlike legs. When moving, it kept three feet on the ground at all times to support its massive weight.

When dinosaur fossils were first discovered in quantity in the early 19th century, they were believed to be the remains of huge, clumsy reptiles. Many people still think that all dinosaurs were massive animals that lumbered along slowly in search of food. In fact, dinosaurs were a very diverse group: although some were enormous, others were not much bigger than hens are today and could run very fast.

An African elephant is 9 ft 2 in (2.8 m) tall.

Average height of an adult human 5 ft 8 in (1.73 m).

Brachiosaurus *height: 39 ft 4 in (12 m)*

Human height: 5 ft 8 in (1.73 m).

Compsognathus *height: 1 ft 4 in (40 cm).*

SMALL AND SPEEDY

At about 3 ft (1 m) long, *Compsognathus* was one of the smallest dinosaurs. Moving quickly on its long hind legs, this agile carnivore darted through vegetation in pursuit of prey such as lizards.

TREE SPACE

As long as a tennis court, and weighing the same as six elephants, *Brachiosaurus* grazed on leaves at the edge of the Jurassic forest. On the forest floor, the tiny *Compsognathus* hunted for insects and lizards.

Powerful jaws armed with razor-sharp teeth

TYRANNOSAURUS REX

With its powerful body and massive head, this fearsome dinosaur was one of the biggest of the meat-eating dinosaurs, and one of the largest carnivorous land animals of all time. *Tyrannosaurus* preyed on plant-eating dinosaurs, some of them larger than itself.

Tyrannosaurus height: 16 ft 5 in (5 m)

Average human height 5 ft 8 in (1.73 m).

17

DINOSAUR BODIES

Like other vertebrates, dinosaurs had a skeleton that supported their body, protected their internal organs, and, with the aid of muscles, enabled them to move. Using bones and teeth preserved as fossils, scientists have been able to rebuild dinosaur skeletons and show what they looked like. As far as their muscles and internal organs are concerned, scientists can only make intelligent guesses.

SKIN IMPRINT
A dinosaur's skin would normally rot quickly after death. This rare fossil dinosaur skin shows that it was tough and scaly. Like the skin of some living reptiles, it was probably also colored and patterned.

Ossified tendons kept the tail stiff.

Bony head-crest

PARASAUROLOPHUS SKELETON
Strong hind limb bones indicate that, like other duck-billed dinosaurs, *Parasaurolophus* usually walked on its hind legs, although it could also feed on all fours. A stiff tail helped it to keep its balance.

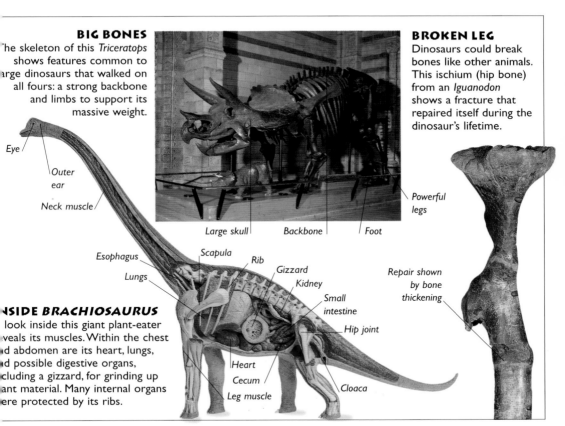

BIG BONES

The skeleton of this *Triceratops* shows features common to large dinosaurs that walked on all fours: a strong backbone and limbs to support its massive weight.

Eye

Outer ear

Neck muscle

Large skull

Backbone

Foot

BROKEN LEG

Dinosaurs could break bones like other animals. This ischium (hip bone) from an *Iguanodon* shows a fracture that repaired itself during the dinosaur's lifetime.

Powerful legs

Repair shown by bone thickening

Esophagus

Scapula

Rib

Lungs

Gizzard

Kidney

Small intestine

Hip joint

INSIDE *BRACHIOSAURUS*

A look inside this giant plant-eater reveals its muscles. Within the chest and abdomen are its heart, lungs, and possible digestive organs, including a gizzard, for grinding up plant material. Many internal organs were protected by its ribs.

Heart

Cecum

Leg muscle

Cloaca

FAST MOVERS

Many types of dinosaur – both carnivores and herbivores – could move fast, either to catch prey or to avoid being caught by a predator. In general, fast movers ran on two legs, had a lightweight body counterbalanced by a long tail, and had long, slender legs. Heavyweight dinosaurs probably moved quickly, but only for short distances. Faster movement evolved at the same time in herbivores and carnivores: as their prey ran faster so did the predators.

DINOSAUR TRACKS
These dinosaur tracks, running up a hillside in Chile, have been preserved for many millions of years. By measuring the distance between one footprint and the next, scientists can calculate how fast the dinosaur was moving.

Powerful legs enable this rhinoceros to charge rapidly over short distances.

HEAVYWEIGHT CHARGERS
Like this modern rhinoceros, some of the big horned dinosaurs, such as *Triceratops*, could charge at an attacking predator. Rhinos can reach speeds up to 28 mph (45 km/h).

QUICK ESCAPE

Always alert to danger as they graze, this herd of Hypsilophodon is frightened by sudden rock fall. They escape at high speed. Living in a herd gave small herbivores greater protection from predators than they would have when living on their own.

SPRINT CHAMPION

Gallimimus was one of the fastest dinosaurs. With a toothless beak, it fed on small animals and fruit. If attacked by larger predators, its only means of escape was to run away at high speed.

Rigid tails helped Hypsilophodon *to balance when running fast.*

UNEVEN RACE

The ostrich has a top running speed of 50 mph (80 km/h). Although the ostrich and *Gallimimus* are not related, they probably had a similar running style. *Gallimimus* may not have run as fast.

Strong, slender hind legs, with long shin and foot bones, enabled Gallimimus *to reach high speeds.*

KEEPING WARM?

To reach the head, high above the body, blood pressure had to be high.

BLOOD FLOW
The current view is that dinosaurs probably had a heart similar to mammals. One side pumped blood at high pressure around the body; the other pumped blood at low pressure to the lungs.

Were dinosaurs warm-blooded like living birds and mammals? Warm-blooded animals maintain a constant internal temperature by digesting food. Or were they cold-blooded, like modern reptiles that depend on the temperature around them to make them active? Studies of dinosaur bones and anatomy suggest they were unique. Young dinosaurs were warm-blooded and grew rapidly; most adults were so large they did not either lose or gain heat from their warm surroundings.

The delicate tissue making up the lungs received blood from the low-pressure circuit.

SOLAR PANELS?

Stegosaurus is easily identifiable from its bony plates. Did they help to keep it warm? Heat from the Sun may have warmed the blood vessels in the skin covering the plates on *Stegosaurus*' back. Its blood supply would then transfer the heat all around its body, enabling it to be active.

Stegosaurus stands in the shallow water of a Jurassic lake.

MAMMAL BONE

This section through horse bone shows the thick, bony cylinders within it. Similar bones were found in some dinosaurs and may show that they were also warm-blooded. Other dinosaurs had bones similar to modern cold-blooded reptiles.

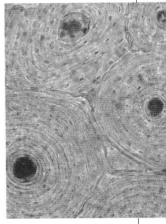

DINOSAUR BONE

This is a section through primary bone from the dinosaur *Cetiosaurus*. Primary bone is formed during rapid growth, and is also found in birds and mammals. This may indicate that dinosaurs were warm-blooded as juveniles when they grew rapidly.

CREST HEAD

Oviraptor (egg thief) had a short head, a hard curved beak, and a toothless jaw that could crush with great pressure. It may have used these jaws to break eggs, or shellfish. The bony crest was probably used to signal to other *Oviraptors*.

STRANGE HEADS

Dinosaur heads showed great variation in shape and size, and may provide clues about their lifestyles. *Troodon's* huge eyes, for example, were ideally suited to a hunter that pursued fast-moving prey. The spikes, crests, and frills found on the heads of some dinosaurs may have been used for defense, to distinguish between females and males, or as signals when rivals competed for territory or mates.

These bony prongs may have been used to crack egg shells.

PSITTACOSAURUS

Psittacosaurus means parrot lizard, a reference to its sharp, parrotlike beak, which it used to snip off tough plant material. *Psittacosaurus* also had small horns on its head and cheeks.

STYGIMOLOCH

Distinctive large head spines and a high-domed head identify the goat-sized *Stygimoloch* (River of Hades Demon). The males of the species competed for mates or territory by running at each other and banging their bony heads together.

TROODON

This small, agile carnivore had large, forward-facing eyes, like those of living hunters, such as cats. These big eyes made it easier to judge when to pounce on fast-moving prey, and may show that *Troodon* hunted at night.

Horns on domed head

CORYTHOSAURUS

Corythosaurus' hollow, bony crest played an important part in communication. It was larger in males than in females and probably patterned, so that individuals could recognize each other within the herd.

These dinosaurs may have been able to call to each other.

PLANT-EATERS

Most dinosaurs were plant-eaters. They needed to eat huge quantities of vegetation every day to stay alive. Long-necked sauropods fed on treetops, stripping off leaves and swallowing them whole. Other herbivores, most with hard beaks, plucked and chewed up tough, low-growing plants. Those dinosaurs with narrow mouths picked out specific plants; those with wide mouths grabbed leaves from a wide variety of plants.

Flexible fifth finger used to hold plants while feeding.

IGUANODON HAND
Iguanodon had particularly versatile hands. If the dinosaur stood on its hind legs and cropped plants with its hard beak, it could grasp stems and leaves with its hands to make feeding easier. When walking on four legs, *Iguanodon's* hoofed fingers formed a "foot."

PRICKLY FOOD
A modern monkey puzzle tree resembles trees that flourished in the age of dinosaurs. Its ancestors' spiky leaves may have deterred dinosaurs. Other plants defended themselves with poisons.

LONG NECK

Brachiosaurus and other long-necked sauropods were the only dinosaurs that could reach up to browse on the treetops. *Brachiosaurus* was the tallest of the sauropods and among the largest dinosaurs to have existed. Its small head at the end of its very long neck was 75 ft (23 m) from the ground.

STOMACH GRINDERS

These are gizzard stones swallowed by sauropods, such as *Brachiosaurus*. These went into their muscular gizzards to help grind up the tons of tough plant food that sauropods consumed daily, making it easier to digest.

Narrow beak used to nip off individual leaves and shoots.

HYPSILOPHODON

Hypsilophodon, a fast-moving herbivore, half as tall as a human, cropped the stems, leaves, and shoots of horsetails and ferns with its narrow beak. The plants were then crushed and pulped by its small teeth before being swallowed.

HERBIVORE TEETH

The teeth of plant-eating dinosaurs varied considerably. Sauropods used teeth at the front of their jaws to cut or rake in leaves. Other plant-eaters cropped off vegetation with their hardened beaks, and chewed it with their cheek teeth before swallowing. These teeth could be in a single row, as in *Iguanodon*, or in several rows, as in *Edmontosaurus*. As the old teeth were worn down, new teeth grew to replace them.

WORN TOOTH
This spoon-shaped tooth comes from *Pelorosaurus*, one of the giant sauropods. The chisel edge of the tooth, with its hard, outer enamel, has been worn away by constantly chopping up plants.

The unworn ridges on the edge of this Iguanodon *tooth show it has been little used.*

RIDGED TOOTH
Iguanodon cropped plants with its beak and then chewed them with its tall, ridged cheek teeth before swallowing. During chewing, a single row of cheek teeth in each jaw met at an angle to grind up food.

Cheek teeth used for chewing.

"Canine" tusk may have been used to threaten rival males.

PERFECT TEETH

Unlike other dinosaurs, *Heterodontosaurus,* this turkey-sized, agile plant-eater had three types of teeth: sharp, upper front teeth that bit against a lower horny pad to crop plants; long "canine" tusks; and tall cheek teeth, for chewing.

EDMONTOSAURUS

Edmontosaurus had a toothless ducklike bill, but it also had up to 1,000 cheek teeth tightly packed in rows in both jaws. The upper jaw was hinged to slide across the lower jaw while chewing.

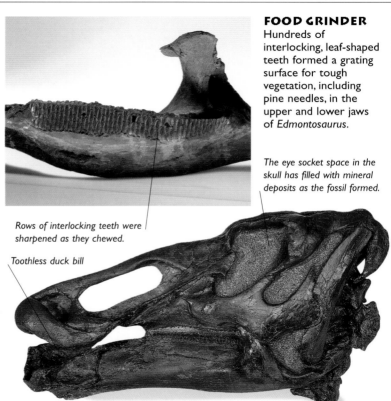

FOOD GRINDER

Hundreds of interlocking, leaf-shaped teeth formed a grating surface for tough vegetation, including pine needles, in the upper and lower jaws of *Edmontosaurus.*

The eye socket space in the skull has filled with mineral deposits as the fossil formed.

Rows of interlocking teeth were sharpened as they chewed.

Toothless duck bill

DEADLY BLADES

Meat-eating dinosaurs used their sharp teeth – and sometimes their claws – to attack and rip open their prey. These carnivores had large heads and long jaws packed with serrated, backward-pointing fangs. These teeth were constantly replaced by new, sharper ones as they wore out. Carnivores could open their jaws very wide to grasp hold of prey, then clamp them tightly shut as they bit. With their teeth locked in a bite, they jerked their heads back to tear out lumps of flesh.

BIG MOUTH

A massive skull, wide, gaping jaws, and large, sharp teeth are typical features of big theropods, such as this *Tyrannosaurus*. Its jaws could bulge outward, so it could bite off and swallow large chunks of meat.

Tiny serrations give the tooth a cutting edge like that of a saw.

GIANT TOOTH

This comparison with a child's hand shows the extraordinary size of the tooth of a *Tyrannosaurus*. Note how its curved edge pointed backward.

NEW TEETH

An inside view of the lower jaw of a hunter from the early Jurassic Period, *Megalosaurus*, shows how teeth were replaced. Throughout a dinosaur's life, new, sharp teeth grew on the inside of old worn-down teeth, which eventually fell out.

New tooth pushing out an old tooth.

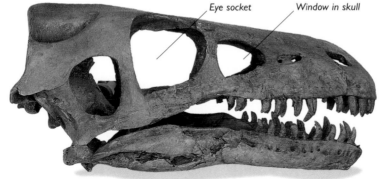

Eye socket   Window in skull

CUTTING EDGE

This small, triangular tooth from *Troodon* shows its sharp serrated edge, similar to that of a steak knife. With 50 teeth in both jaws, *Troodon* was well armed for killing lizards and small mammals.

DROMAEOSAURUS SKULL

Large openings in this hunter's skull helped to make it lighter. The central opening is the eye socket; powerful jaw muscles passed through the other openings.

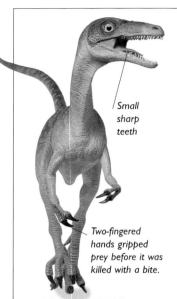

Small sharp teeth

Two-fingered hands gripped prey before it was killed with a bite.

HUNTING ALONE

Carnivorous dinosaurs needed keen eyesight and sharp teeth. They were skilled predators, and all of them were theropods. Most of them hunted alone. Among the large theropods, *Allosaurus* and *Tyrannosaurus* usually preyed on large plant-eating dinosaurs. They probably stalked herds of herbivores, getting as close as possible, before attacking. Small theropods, such as *Troodon* and the hen-sized *Compsognathus*, caught small fast prey.

AGILE HUNTER

Compsognathus was a small, speedy predator that chased lizards, large insects, and perhaps small mammals. Its streamlined shape enabled it to run through dense undergrowth.

ALLOSAURUS ATTACK

The large theropod *Allosaurus* is attacking a young *Diplodocus* in this late Jurassic scene. *Allosaurus* may have set upon this animal because it had strayed from the herd. It attacked by sinking its teeth into the herbivore's flesh.

SMALL PREY

Dragonflies, like this one, are ancient insects that first appeared long before the age of dinosaurs and still exist today. They may have been eaten by *Compsognathus*.

High-speed sprinting may not be enough to save the smaller dinosaur.

Troodon had the largest brain for its size of any dinosaur.

GAPING JAWS

Tyrannosaurus charges, its jaws open to reveal its arsenal of sharp teeth. The small dinosaur fleeing before the charging *Tyrannosaurus* is *Struthiomimus*. The intended victim may be a large herbivore or possibly this is one of a pair of battling *Tyrannosaurus* rivals.

BIG-EYED TROODON

Fast-moving *Troodon* hunted small mammals, dinosaurs, and lizards. This turkey-sized dinosaur had small razor-sharp teeth and long arms and legs. Its large, forward-facing eyes helped it to judge how far away its prey was before pouncing.

Sharp claws on each three-fingered hand were used for grasping prey.

PACK HUNTERS

READY TO ATTACK
Deinonychus was about the same size as an adult man, and was probably the largest of the pack-hunting dinosaurs. This *Deinonychus* skeleton is in a leaping position, its limbs and deadly claws outstretched and its jaws wide open, ready to bite.

Some smaller carnivorous dinosaurs hunted in packs to attack prey larger than themselves. Lightly built and agile, they had grasping hands and a large switchblade claw on each foot for slashing their victims. Their jaws were armed with saw-edged teeth to tear flesh. These dinosaurs also had long legs so they could run fast, excellent vision, and long, stiff tails that helped them to keep their balance.

Tail kept rigid by bony rods along the vertebrae.

This claw was held upright to protect its sharp edge when walking.

The curved claws act as hooks.

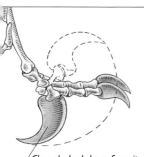

Claw slashed down from its upright resting position.

TERRIBLE CLAW

A close-up view of a *Deinonychus'* foot shows the large, sickle-shaped claw on its second toe. When *Deinonychus* attacked, the toe swiveled down to slash its prey like a knife blade.

Tenontosaurus *collapses under the relentless attack of a pack of* Deinonychus.

GANG BASHING

A pack of *Deinonychus* attack a horse-sized *Tenontosaurus*. They leap onto it and slash at its tough hide with their claws. Weakened by blood loss, the *Tenontosaurus* sinks to the ground. The *Deinonychus* start to tear into their prey, hastening its death.

TEAM WORK

Some modern meat-eating mammals hunt in packs to kill prey larger than themselves, in much the same way that smaller carnivorous dinosaurs did. These African hyenas feed together on the carcass of a large grazing animal, killed by teamwork.

SIZE MATTERS

Size provided an effective defense for the largest herbivores, such as this *Brachiosaurus*, against even the largest predators. At 75 ft (23 m) long, an adult *Brachiosaurus* would dwarf a modern-day lion. A persistent attacker could have been knocked aside by the *Brachiosaurus'* huge whiplike tail.

Brachiosaurus

Lion

ON THE DEFENSE

Plant-eating dinosaurs were constantly at risk of being attacked and eaten by carnivorous dinosaurs, so over time they developed various defenses. The ankylosaurs had armored skin and spines, the ceratopians wielded horns and bony neck frills, and the sauropods depended on their huge size and whiplash tails. Centrosaurs herded together for protection, while dinosaurs that ran on their hind legs relied on speed or camouflage to escape from predators.

SAFETY IN NUMBERS

Living in a herd provided protection for many herbivorous dinosaurs. A group of *Centrosaurus* would gather around younger members of the herd, their long horns pointing outward, to ward off predators.

HORNED DEFENSE

The massive body, large neck frill, and long, bony horns of *Triceratops* may have been enough to put off potential attackers. But if a large predator, such as *Tyrannosaurus*, did attack, *Triceratops* could defend itself by inflicting fatal wounds with a single thrust of its three-horned head.

TOUGH OUTSIDE

A modern mammal, the armadillo (above), rolls up so that only its tough skin is exposed. The armored dinosaur *Hylaeosaurus* probably lay down, so only its armored skin was exposed.

SPINY DEFENSE

In the early Cretaceous Period there was a group of dinosaurs, the ankylosaurs, that were like living tanks. Bony plates in their skin and spines on their sides provided armorlike protection.

Sharp spines stuck out along each side of the body to prevent an attacker from reaching the soft underbelly.

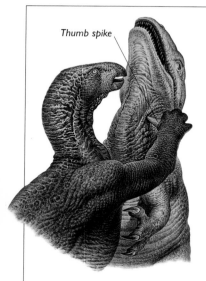
Thumb spike

WEAPONS

Some herbivorous dinosaurs had weapons to defend themselves from attacks by carnivorous dinosaurs. These included the bone-crushing, clubbed tail of *Euoplocephalus* and the stabbing thumb spike of *Iguanodon*. These weapons did not necessarily kill the attacker, but wounded or disabled it so that the herbivore was left alone. A wounded predator may have been so badly hurt that it could not feed and died from starvation.

STABBING WEAPON
When attacked by a large predator, *Iguanodon* fought back. On each hand it had a large, bony thumb spike. *Iguanodon* reared up on its hind legs and stabbed its thumb spike into the attacking dinosaur's flesh.

BONY CLUB
This fossilized tail club provided *Euoplocephalus* with a very dangerous heavy weapon. The club consisted of four bony plates attached to the bones at the end of the dinosaur's swinging tail.

BONE CRUSHER

Like other ankylosaurs, *Euoplocephalus* had protective armor covering its head and back. It could also defend itself by swinging its heavy tail club against an attacker, delivering a bone-breaking blow.

Bony club at the end of the tail

Dorsal plates

Two pairs of sharp tail spines stab from side-to-side.

SPIKED DEFENSE

The plated dinosaur *Stegosaurus* had both dorsal plates and a dangerously spiked tail. It was the size of a modern bus but still vulnerable to attack. Its spiky tail could stab and cripple a predator.

BATTLING MALES

Carnivorous dinosaurs used their sharp claws and teeth to kill prey. They may also have used these weapons when competing with their own species. These two *Deinonychus* males may be fighting over territory or females.

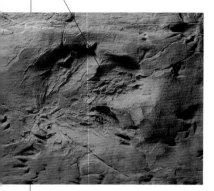

Large predator's footprint

SOCIAL LIFE

Plant-eating dinosaurs lived together in herds. Evidence for this comes from fossilized footprints that show many dinosaurs moving together, and from comparisons with modern herbivores that live in herds, such as antelope. Living in a herd provided safety in numbers, especially for young dinosaurs. Some animals could stand guard while others fed or rested.

HERD FOOTPRINTS

Preserved footprints, such as these from Australia, provide evidence that dinosaurs lived in herds. The central footprint, that of a large predator, is overrun by those of smaller dinosaurs. The herd probably stampeded past the approaching hunter.

Long, sound-producing crest

The crest may have also acted as a visual signal.

SNORKEL HEAD

Some duck-billed dinosaurs, such as *Parasaurolophus*, had a hollow crest. When air was forced from the lungs through the tubes and chambers inside the crest, they vibrated and made sounds. These sounds could have identified an individual or warned of danger.

WILDEBEEST HERD

These modern herbivores, from Africa, live in herds. Predators have to creep up close, without being spotted, before attacking animals on the edge of the herd.

HEAD-BUTTING

These two male *Pachycephalosaurus* are probably competing for mates and territory by banging their heads together.

ON THE LOOKOUT

In a scene from the late Cretaceous in North America, three groups of hadrosaurs, or duck-billed dinosaurs, and their young feed and rest near water. Some herd members are on the lookout to warn the others that a predator is approaching.

Thick bone provided a battering ram as rival males clashed.

A domed skull was typical of the "bone-headed" dinosaurs.

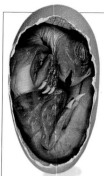

Oviraptor egg

Hen egg

DINOSAUR BABIES

Dinosaurs laid eggs, just as modern reptiles and birds do. Fossil eggs have been found in hollows scooped out of soil or sand. Nests were often grouped together for protection. Dinosaur eggs were small, even when the adults were large. The shells of large eggs would have been too thick to let oxygen pass to the baby dinosaur inside, or to crack during hatching.

EGG SIZE
This model of an *Oviraptor* egg with an embryo inside it shows that it is only about twice the length of a modern hen's egg, yet the adult *Oviraptor* was about 6 ft (1.8 m) long.

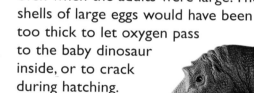

CARING MOM
Females of the duck-billed dinosaur *Maiasaura* (good mother lizard) returned to the same nesting sites each year, where they laid up to 20 eggs. The mothers fed and protected the young until they were big enough to find food for themselves.

MAIASAURA NURSERY

Young *Maiasaura* were too small and weak to leave the nest after hatching. Other dinosaur hatchlings were strong enough to leave the nest immediately after hatching. Only a few probably survived to become adults.

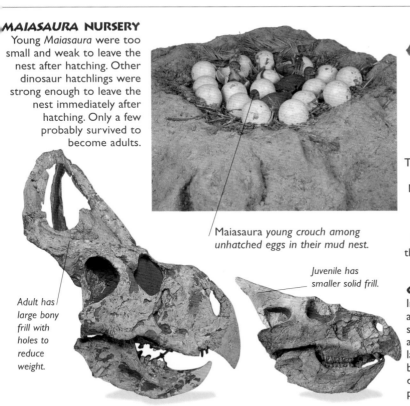

Maiasaura *young crouch among unhatched eggs in their mud nest.*

Adult has large bony frill with holes to reduce weight.

Juvenile has smaller solid frill.

EGG SHELL

These pieces of *Oviraptor* egg shell were found in Mongolia. The bumps on them prevented tiny pores (openings) in the shell from becoming blocked. Oxygen passed through the pores to the developing dinosaurs.

GROWING HEADS

In some dinosaurs, such as *Protoceratops*, their skull shape changed with age. The adult skull had a larger bony frill at the back of the skull, used for display and to secure the powerful jaw muscles.

43

DISCOVERING DINOSAURS

Dinosaur fossils have been found for thousands of years, but it was not until the 19th century that the formal study of dinosaurs began. In the 1820s English fossil hunters described finds of extinct giant reptiles, and in 1841 these were named dinosaurs. The hunt for dinosaurs spread to the United States, and later to the rest of the world. Many mistakes were made at first in piecing together dinosaurs' anatomy and lifestyles.

DR. GIDEON MANTELL (1790-1852)

An English doctor and keen fossil hunter, Gideon Mantell and his wife discovered large reptile teeth and bones near a quarry in 1822. In 1825 Mantell named his find *Iguanodon*.

DRAWING DINOSAURS

In 1834, a partial skeleton of *Iguanodon* was discovered in a quarry. Bought by friends of Gideon Mantell, the fossil hunter, it enabled him to produce his first sketch of the dinosaur.

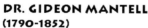

Iguanodon bones embedded in a slab of rock.

LIVING IN TREES?

When fossils of *Hypsilophodon* were first discovered, it was thought to have lived in trees, gripping the branches with its toes as shown here. We now know *Hypsilophodon* lived on the ground, where its long-toed feet made it a fast runner.

STUDYING FOSSILS

Paleontologists — scientists who study fossils — carefully remove fossilized remains of a dinosaur from the ground and send them back to the museum for study.

SIR RICHARD OWEN (1804-92)

An expert on animal anatomy at London's Natural History Museum, when examining giant reptile fossils, he realized that they were unlike any living species. In 1841 he named them dinosaurs, meaning terrible lizards.

R. C. ANDREWS (1884-1960)

An explorer, he led the first American dinosaur-hunting expedition to the Gobi Desert in Mongolia. The team discovered several species and, in 1922, the first dinosaur eggs to be found: those of *Oviraptor*.

DINOSAUR FOSSILS

Fossils form when dead animals are rapidly covered by sediment, such as sand or silt. Their soft parts decay, leaving behind hard parts such as teeth and bones. In time, minerals seep into the hard parts to form rocky replicas of the original structures, called fossils. After millions of years, erosion by wind, water, or quarrying exposes the fossils.

How has so much been discovered about dinosaurs when they have been extinct for millions of years? Most of the evidence comes from preserved remains called fossils, as well as clues from living dinosaur relations, such as reptiles and birds. Fossilization takes place when an animal's hard parts, such as teeth and bone, are buried and are partly replaced by rock. Some eggs, nests, and droppings have also been preserved as fossils.

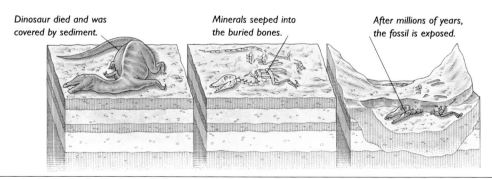

Dinosaur died and was covered by sediment.

Minerals seeped into the buried bones.

After millions of years, the fossil is exposed.

FOSSIL DROPPINGS

These are fossilized animal droppings, known as coprolites. They were probably deposited by a large sauropod called *Titanosaurus* that lived in India in the late Cretaceous.

Plant remains can be seen on the surface.

FOSSIL EGGS

This fossilized sandy nest shows the eggs exactly as they were laid in a spiral pattern by a female *Oviraptor* about 80 mya.

Jawbone and massive flesh-tearing teeth

TOOTH BRUSHING

Paleontologist Rodolfo Coria is cleaning the teeth on the fossil jawbone of *Gigantosaurus*, a giant carnivore discovered in South America in 1993. At 41 ft (12.5 m) long, it was bigger than *Tyrannosaurus*.

RUNNING FOOT

These are the fossilized foot bones of *Albertosaurus*, a large carnivore that lived in the late Cretaceous. The upper foot bones are joined together to make the foot strong enough to support the dinosaur's weight.

Upper foot bones fused together

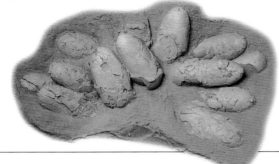

RE-CREATING DINOSAURS

Working out the structure of a dinosaur from its fossilized remains is a skilled and time-consuming task. After carefully excavating the site where the fossil is found, the remains are jacketed in plaster of Paris or polyurethane foam to protect them on their journey to a museum. There, the protective jacket is removed and the bones are cleaned. Fiberglass casts are then made of the bones and assembled into a skeleton.

FOSSIL FIND

A team from a museum excavates the fossil bones of *Baryonyx*, a newly discovered fish-eating theropod. The find was made following the discovery of a single claw by an amateur fossil hunter in 1983.

CLEANING

In a museum laboratory, the dinosaur fossils are thoroughly cleaned and any surrounding rock removed. The bones can then be studied by experts, who will classify them and publish any new information about the find.

DEATH POSE

This model of *Baryonyx* shows how it probably looked shortly after dying. Its bones were fossilized in this position at the bottom of a lake. A reconstruction may involve experts on fossils, plants, rocks, and animal anatomy as well as the skill of a model maker.

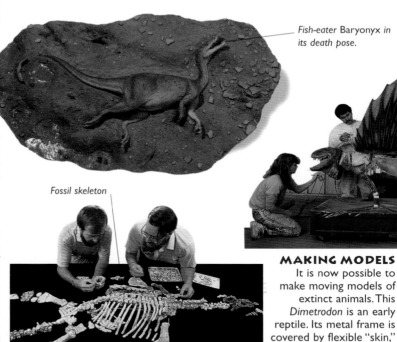

Fish-eater Baryonyx *in its death pose.*

Fossil skeleton

PIECING TOGETHER

Two paleontologists put together the skeleton of a plesiosaur from fossil remains. Plesiosaurs were sea-dwelling, carnivorous reptiles that lived at the same time as dinosaurs. The bones are pale pink because the original bone material has been replaced by opal.

MAKING MODELS

It is now possible to make moving models of extinct animals. This *Dimetrodon* is an early reptile. Its metal frame is covered by flexible "skin," and it is moved by a computer. Similar models of dinosaurs are made.

EARLY BIRDS

DINOSAUR OR BIRD

This fossil of *Archaeopteryx* was discovered in a German quarry in 1877. It had a long tail, spiky teeth, and clawed fingers like a dinosaur, but feathers, long arms, and a wishbone like a bird.

Most scientists who study fossils agree that birds evolved from small theropod dinosaurs that lived in the late Jurassic Period. Fossils of pigeon-sized *Archaeopteryx*, the earliest known bird, which lived about 147 mya, show that it had both dinosaur and bird features. Other fossils of early birds, such as *Confuciusornis,* discovered recently in China, show how modern birds evolved. No one knows definitely how birds developed the ability to fly.

GROUND UP THEORY

This theory suggests that small therapod dinosaurs evolved feathered fringes on their arms. Flapping their arms enabled these bird ancestors to leap into the air to chase insects in flight. Wings and flapping flight developed later as a result of this.

CHASING PREY

Archaeopteryx glides above the floor of a coniferous forest in pursuit of flying insects. The shape and arrangement of its feathers indicate that *Archaeopteryx* flew rather clumsily.

Dragonflies may have been the prey of Archaeopteryx.

The legs of giant sauropod resemble tree trunks.

TREES DOWN THEORY

This theory suggests the appearance of feathers enabled tree-living bird ancestors to parachute to the ground. Wings came later, enabling early birds to glide from tree to tree and eventually to fly.

Preserved feathers around the arms and tail

CONFUCIUSORNIS

These two fossils of *Confuciusornis* look more like modern birds than *Archaeopteryx*, since they have beaks instead of teeth, lightweight jaws, and stubby tails. However, they are not thought to be the direct ancestors of modern birds.

END OF THE DINOSAURS

Dinosaurs dominated life on land for 160 million years, adapting successfully to many changes in their surroundings. Yet 65 mya, they became extinct, along with flying and marine reptiles. Why this happened, no one is really sure. Possible explanations include a large asteroid colliding with the Earth, great volcanic activity, or gradual climate change. Whatever the cause, the dinosaurs were unable to adapt, and they disappeared.

VOLCANIC ACTIVITY

Many volcanoes were active at the end of the Cretaceous. Erupting volcanoes release carbon dioxide gas that can cause dramatic climate change. Poisonous volcanic dust could have penetrated dinosaurs' eggs.

SINGLE SEX EGGS

Whether these crocodile hatchlings are male or female depends on the temperature at which they were incubated. If the same was true of dinosaur eggs, climate change may have resulted in dinosaurs of only one sex hatching.

ASTEROID STRIKE

An asteroid 6 miles (10 km) across may have hit the Earth 65 mya. The impact would have thrown dust into the atmosphere, blocking out sunlight and causing cold, stormy weather. The dinosaurs could not have survived this change of climate.

ulated by their fur, small mammals d survive a cold, dark global winter.

DINOSAUR SURVIVORS

Birds are feathered, warm-blooded descendants of the theropod dinosaurs. With over 9,700 species, found almost everywhere on Earth, birds are perhaps the most successful of all dinosaurs.

Modern birds, such as this magpie, are the direct descendants of small, meat-eating dinosaurs called theropods.

CLIMATE CHANGE

At the end of the Cretaceous, the climate was cool and wet. Plants became less abundant. Without food, the herbivorous dinosaurs and the carnivorous dinosaurs that hunted them became extinct.

INDEX

Heterodontosaurus

A

Oviraptor
nest

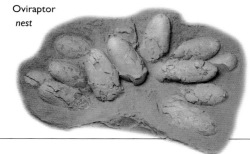

Young Protoceratop's *skull*

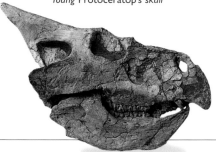

Euoplocephalus'
tail club

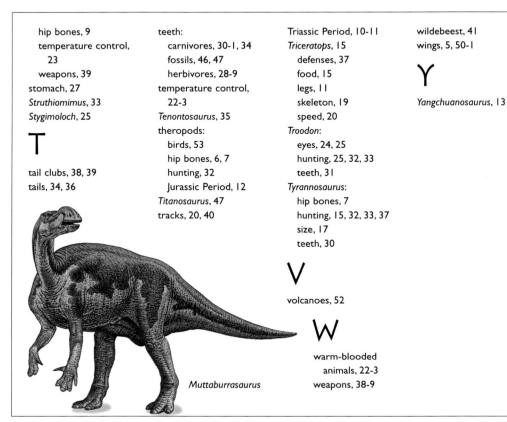

Muttaburrasaurus